SQUASH

TURNIP

EGGPLANT

CORN

RADISH

BROCCOLI

PEA

VEGETABLES in HOLIDAY UNDERWEAR

JARED CHAPMAN

ABRAMS APPLESEED, NEW YORK

FOR
HAYES, ARLIE & LUKE

CATALOGING-IN-PUBLICATION DATA HAS BEEN APPLIED FOR AND MAY BE OBTAINED FROM THE LIBRARY OF CONGRESS. ISBN 978-1-4197-3654-4. COPYRIGHT © 2019 JARED CHAPMAN. BOOK DESIGN BY CHAD W. BECKERMAN. PUBLISHED IN 2019 BY ABRAMS APPLESEED, AN IMPRINT OF ABRAMS. ALL RIGHTS RESERVED. NO PORTION OF THIS BOOK MAY BE REPRODUCED, STORED IN A RETRIEVAL SYSTEM, OR TRANSMITTED IN ANY FORM OR BY ANY MEANS, MECHANICAL, ELECTRONIC, PHOTOCOPYING, RECORDING, OR OTHERWISE, WITHOUT WRITTEN PERMISSION FROM THE PUBLISHER. ABRAMS APPLESEED® IS A REGISTERED TRADEMARK OF HARRY N. ABRAMS, INC. FOR BULK DISCOUNT INQUIRIES, CONTACT SPECIALSALES@ABRAMSBOOKS.COM. PRINTED AND BOUND IN CHINA 10 9 8 7 6 5 4 3 2 1

ABRAMS The Art of Books
195 Broadway, New York, NY 10007
abramsbooks.com

I'VE BEEN WAITING

JANUARY

FEBRUARY

MARCH

JULY

AUGUST

SEPTEMBER

ALL YEAR LONG . . .

APRIL

MAY

JUNE

OCTOBER

NOVEMBER

FOR HOLIDAY UNDERWEAR SEASON!

UM . . . WHAT'S THAT?

IT'S THE MOST WONDERFUL TIME OF THE YEAR!

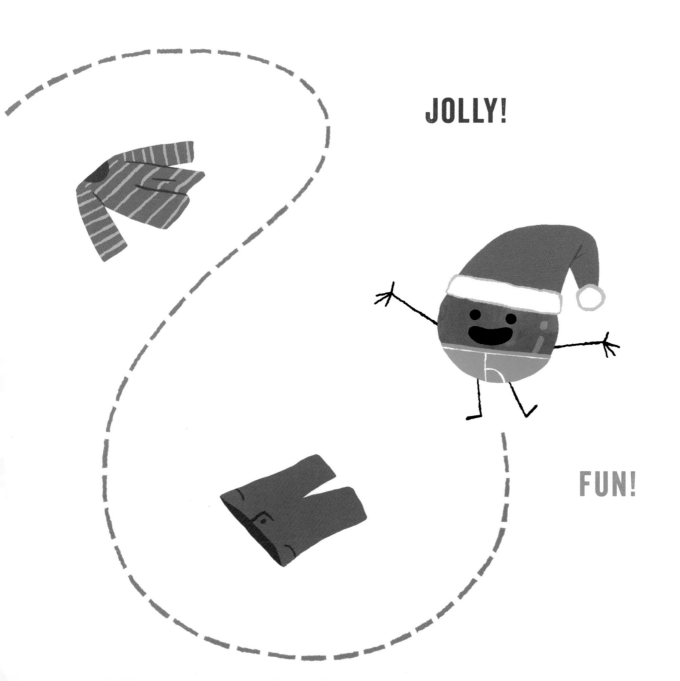

JOLLY!

FUN!

THERE'S COZY UNDERWEAR

AND SCRATCHY UNDERWEAR,

INSIDE UNDERWEAR AND

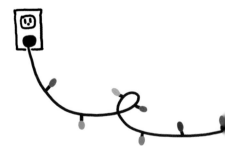

OUTSIDE **UNDERWEAR,**

STRETCHY UNDERWEAR

AND TIGHT UNDERWEAR!

THERE'S UNDERWEAR THAT'S THE SAME

THERE'S UNDERWEAR FOR BEING
ALONE

AND UNDERWEAR FOR BEING TOGETHER.

WAIT A SECOND . . .

BUT HOLIDAY UNDERWEAR
IS FOR EVERYONE!

FINE.

MAYBE YOU AREN'T READY YET.

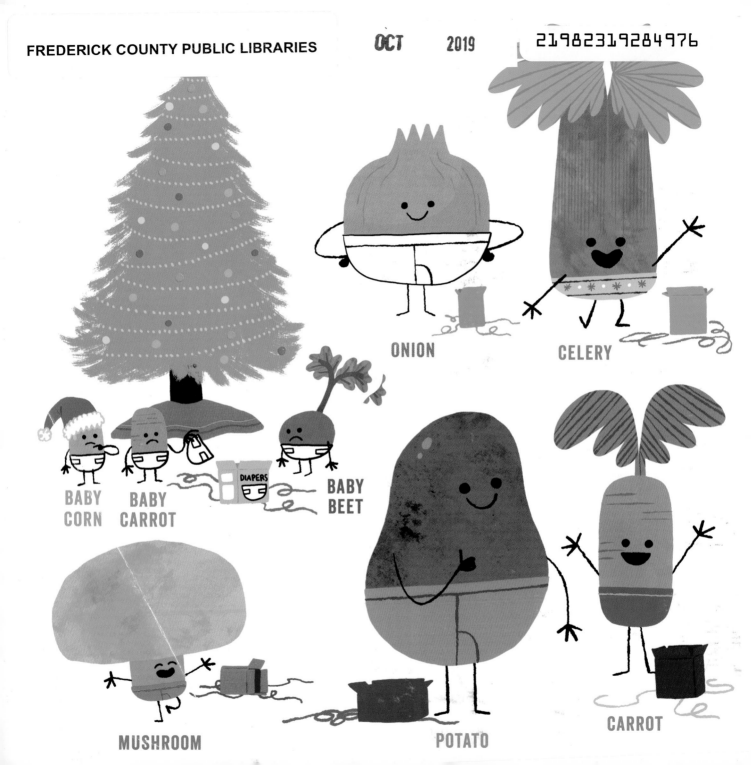